Dancing

A Richard Jackson Book

Dancing

Denys Cazet

with music by Craig Bond

Orchard Books · New York

Alex slammed the screen door and stuck out his tongue at the stars.

He could hear the new baby crying.

"What a *whaa whaa* baby," he muttered, covering his ears.

Alex's father sat down next to him. "I put some of my favorite music on," he said. "Very romantic . . . perfect for a summer evening."

"Too much screaming," said Alex. "I can't hear."

"Maybe you should take your hands away from your ears."

Alex uncovered one ear. "Maybe we can send the baby back to the hospital. He's almost new."

Alex's father opened his wallet. He showed Alex a pink piece of paper. "Paid in full," he said. "We own him."

"Oh," sighed Alex.

Father turned and looked at the house. "It's very quiet in there. I think Mama is rocking the baby to sleep."

"Now I can hear the music," said Alex. "But I don't hear any words."

"I remember the words," said his father. "I think this song is about you."

"Can you sing it?"

Father nodded. He listened a moment and then sang:

*"Maybe it's me,
maybe it's you,
but something is wrong.
Is there somebody new?
Go ahead, tell me,
because . . . I love you. I love you."*

"Somebody new in diapers,"
said Alex.

*"Maybe it's me,
maybe it's you.
There must be a reason
for feeling so blue.
Go ahead, tell me,
because . . . I love you.
I love you."*

"B—A—B—Y," spelled Alex.

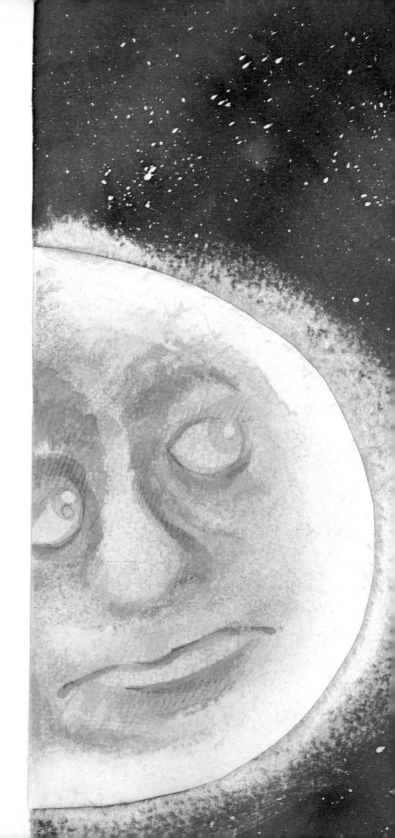

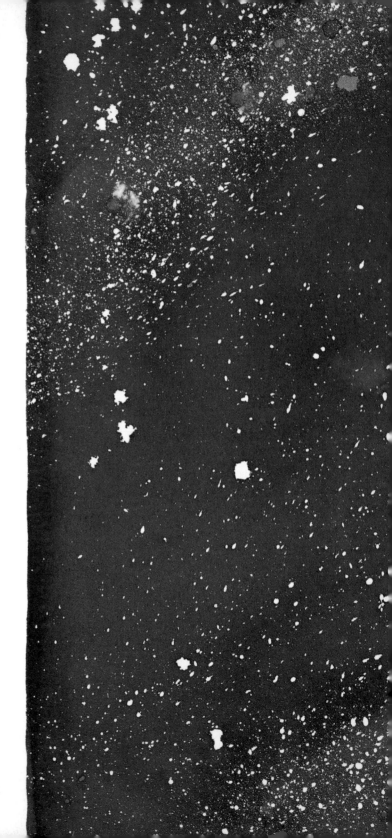

"Maybe the moon
knows just how you feel,
sharing the night
with the stars.
They'll be dancing forever
through all the heavens,
dancing forever and ever.

"Maybe it's me,
Maybe it's you.
So come dance with me
under an indigo sky,
and I'll whisper forever,
I love you. I love you."

Alex stared at the stars.

"Will you dance with me?" Alex asked.

Father bowed. "My pleasure."
He picked Alex up. They danced
beneath the summer stars. They
danced beneath the moon.

Alex held tight. "What if I fall?"
"Then, I'll catch you."
"Always?" asked Alex.
"Always," said his father.

Always.

For Jack,
another star

Orchard Books, 95 Madison Avenue, New York, NY 10016

Manufactured in the United States of America
Printed by Barton Press, Inc. Bound by Horowitz/Rae.
Book design by Mina Greenstein. The text of this book is set in 16 point Adobe
Versailles. The illustrations are pencil and watercolor drawings
reproduced in full color.
10 9 8 7 6 5 4 3 2 1

Library of Congress Cataloging-in-Publication Data
Cazet, Denys.
Dancing / by Denys Cazet ; with music by Craig Bond.
p.   cm. "A Richard Jackson book"—Half t.p.
Summary: Alex's father sings a song to reassure him that he is still loved, even though
there is a new baby in the family.
ISBN 0-531-09466-9.   ISBN 0-531-08766-2 (lib. bdg.)
[1. Babies—Fiction.   2. Fathers and sons—Fiction.]   I. Bond, Craig, ill.   II. Title.
PZ7.C2985Dan   1995   [E]—dc20   94-45920